For Davy
—B.F.

For Ken
—S.A.

Tricycle Press
an imprint of Ten Speed Press
PO Box 7123
Berkeley, California 94707
www.tricyclepress.com

Design by Florence Ma
Typeset in Chaparral Pro and Calligraphic 421 BT
The illustrations in this book were rendered in gouache.

Library of Congress Cataloging-in-Publication Data

Franco, Betsy.
 Zero Is the Leaves On the Tree/ by Betsy Franco ;
illustrations by Shino Arihara.
  p. cm.
 Includes bibliographical references and index.
 ISBN-13: 978-1-58246-249-3 (hardcover : alk. paper)
 ISBN-10: 1-58246-249-6 (hardcover : alk. paper)
 1. Zero (The number)--Juvenile literature.
 I. Arihara, Shino, 1973- ill.
 II. Title.
 QA141.3.F734 2009
 513--dc22
                                   2008042185

First Tricycle Press printing, 2009
Printed in China

1 2 3 4 5 6 — 13 12 11 10 09

Zero Is
the Leaves
on the Tree

by BETSY FRANCO

illustrations by SHINO ARIHARA

TRICYCLE PRESS
Berkley / Toronto

Zero is...

the shape of an egg.

Zero is a number.

Zero is...

the balls in the bin at recess time.

0 balls

Zero is...

the leaves on the bare,

brown arms of the oak tree.

0 leaves

Zero is...

the ducks on the pond when
the air says winter is coming.

0 ducks

Zero is...

the sound of snowflakes
　　　　landing on your mitten.

0 sounds

Zero is...

the sleds on the hillside
when the snow turns to slush.

0 sleds

Zero is...

the kites in the

sky once the wind stops blowing.

0 kites

Zero is...

the blossoms in the garden
just before the buds open.

0 blossoms

0 bikes

Zero is...

the bikes in the bike rack
on the last day of school.

Zero is...

the ripples in the pool

before the first swimmer jumps in.

0 ripples

Zero is...

the footprints on the beach

when the waves come in and in and in.

0 footprints

Zero is...

the sound of stars filling the night.